What's in the Pond, Dear Dragon?

by Margaret Hillert

Illustrated by David Schimmell

NORWOOD HOUSE PRESS

DEAR CAREGIVER, The *Beginning-to-Read* series is a carefully written collection of classic readers you may remember from your own childhood. Each book features text comprised of common sight words to provide your child ample practice reading the words that appear most frequently in written text. The many additional details in the pictures enhance the story and offer the opportunity for you to help your child expand oral language and develop comprehension.

Begin by reading the story to your child, followed by letting him or her read familiar words and soon your child will be able to read the story independently. At each step of the way, be sure to praise your reader's efforts to build his or her confidence as an independent reader. Discuss the pictures and encourage your child to make connections between the story and his or her own life. At the end of the story, you will find reading activities and a word list that will help your child practice and strengthen beginning reading skills.

Above all, the most important part of the reading experience is to have fun and enjoy it!

Shannon Cannon

Shannon Cannon,
Literacy Consultant

Norwood House Press • P.O. Box 316598 • Chicago, Illinois 60631
For more information about Norwood House Press please visit our website at
www.norwoodhousepress.com or call 866-565-2900.

LIBRARY OF CONGRESS CATALOGING-IN-PUBLICATION DATA
    Hillert, Margaret.
     What's in the pond, dear dragon? / by Margaret Hillert ; illustrated by
David Schimmell.
       pages cm -- (A beginning-to-read book)
     Summary:"A boy and his pet dragon go exploring at a nearby pond.
They learn about fish, plants, and boats that can be found in ponds. This
title includes reading activities and a word list"—Provided by publisher.
     ISBN 978-1-59953-607-1 (library edition : alk. paper)
     ISBN 978-1-60357-602-4 (ebook)
     [1. Ponds--Fiction. 2. Nature--Fiction. 3. Dragons--Fiction.] I.
Schimmell, David, illustrator. II. Title. III. Title: What is in the pond, dear dragon?
     PZ7.H558Wf 2013
     [E]--dc23

                   2013010283

Manufactured in the United States of America in North Mankato, Minnesota.
233N—072013

A pond is a lot of water.

Pretty flowers grow here.
Yellow and white flowers.

Here are some that look like cat tails.

WOW!
Look at that big turtle in the sand.

Look at the eggs and the little,
little babies.
The babies run to the pond.

What about this?
See this big frog.
I will put it down.

It can hop, hop, hop.
It is good at that.

Come here now.
Look way, way down!

Oh Father, I can see some fish.
Big fish and little fish.

There is one like we have at home.

Here is something green for it to eat.

Do you want to eat?
Mother made something for us to eat.

Oh yes.
That will be good.
Then can we play ball?

Yes, Yes.
It will be good to do that.

Here it comes.
Run, run to get it.

I hurt my knee.

Let me see it.

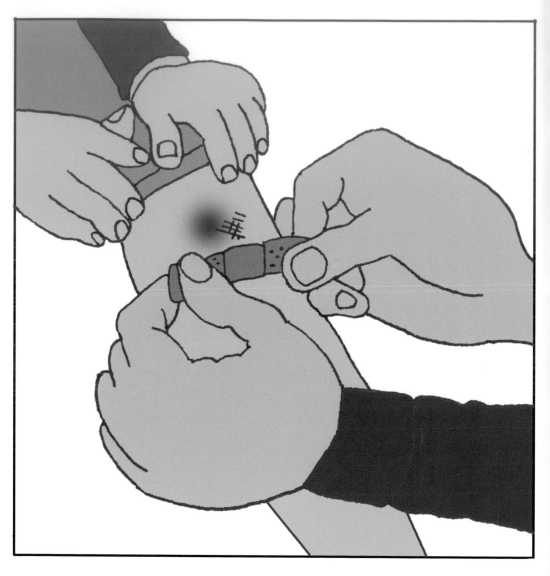

This will help.

I feel better.
Let's look for more things.

Look at the little red boat, Father.

That is a canoe.
We can ride in it. Hop in, hop in.

Oh, boy! This is fun.
Make it go Father, make it go!

Now we are in the pond.
Here I am with you.

And here you are with me.
Oh what fun, Dear Dragon.

READING REINFORCEMENT

The following activities support the findings of the National Reading Panel that determined the most effective components for reading instruction are: Phonemic Awareness, Phonics, Vocabulary, Fluency, and Text Comprehension.

Phonemic Awareness: The /p/ sound

Substitution: Ask your child to say the following words without the /p/ sound:

pat - /p/ = at	pop - /p/ = op	Pam - /p/ = am
pit - /p/ = it	peel - /p/ = eel	pant - /p/ = ant
pair - /p/ = air	pin - /p/ = in	

Phonics: The letter Nn

1. Demonstrate how to form the letters **N** and **n** for your child.

2. Have your child practice writing **N** and **n** at least three times each.

3. Ask your child to point to the words in the book that have the letter **n**.

4. Write down the following words and ask your child to circle the letter **n** in each word:

and	fun	can	down	now
then	something	want	one	canoe
pond	sand	run	green	noon
run	nut			

Vocabulary: Animal Names

1. Ask your child to name the animals in the story. Write the words on separate pieces of paper.

   Turtle   Frog   Fish

2. Read each word to your child and ask your child to repeat it.

3. Mix the words up. Point to a word and ask your child to read it. Provide clues if your child needs them.

4. Mix the words up again. Read the following sentences to your child. Ask your child to point to the word described in the sentence:

   • Name the animal in the story that was in the sand. (turtle)

   • Which animal in the story is one you could have as a pet living in your house? (fish, frog, or turtle)

   • What animal hops? (frog)

Fluency: Echo Reading

1. Reread the story to your child at least two more times while your child tracks the print by running a finger under the words as they are read. Ask your child to read the words he or she knows with you.

2. Reread the story, stopping after each sentence or page to allow your child to read (echo) what you have read. Repeat echo reading and let your child take the lead.

Text Comprehension: Discussion Time

1. Ask your child to retell the sequence of events in the story.

2. To check comprehension, ask your child the following questions:

   • What did they find in the pond?

   • What is the little red boat called?

   • What kind of things do the boy and Father do at the pond?

   • In the story, fish eat plants. What is your favorite thing to eat?

***What's in the Pond, Dear Dragon?* uses the 94 words listed below.**

The **7** words bolded below serve as an introduction to new vocabulary, while the other 87 are pre-primer. You may wish to write the words on index cards and use them to help your child build automatic word recognition. Regular practice with these words will enhance your child's fluency in reading connected text.

a	eat	I	play	us
about	eggs	is	pond	
am		in	pretty	want
and		it	put	way
are	Father			**water**
at	feel			we
	fish	knee	red	what
	flowers		ride	white
ball	for	let('s)	run	will
babies	frog	like		with
be	fun	little	**sand**	
better		look	see	**wow**
big		lot	some	
boat	get		something	yellow
boy	go	made		yes
	good	make		you
	green	me	tails	
can	grow	more	that	
canoe		Mother	the	
cat	have	my	then	
come(s)	help		there	
	here		things	
dear	home	now	this	
do	**hop**		to	
down	hurt	of	**turtle**	
dragon		oh		
		one		

ABOUT THE AUTHOR

Margaret Hillert has written over 80 books for children who are just learning to read. Her books have been translated into many different languages and over a million children throughout the world have read her books. She first started writing poetry as a child and has continued to write for children and adults throughout her life. A first grade teacher for 34 years, Margaret is now retired from teaching and lives in Michigan where she likes to write, take walks in the morning, and care for her three cats.

Photograph by Glenna Washburn

ABOUT THE ILLUSTRATOR

David Schimmell served as a professional firefighter for 23 years before hanging up his boots and helmet to devote himself to working as an illustrator of children's books. David has happily created illustrations for the New Dear Dragon books as well as other artwork for educational and retail book projects. Born and raised in Evansville, Indiana, he lives there today with his wife and family.